The Story of

LENGTHWISE

The Story of LENGTHWISE

By

Ernestine Cobern Beyer

illustrated by Don Madden

Follett Publishing Company
Chicago

LIBRARY OF CONGRESS CATALOG CARD NUMBER: 67-17285

ISBN 0-695-48360-9 Titan binding
ISBN 0-695-88360-7 Trade binding
Fourth printing

Dedicated to my son-in-law,
Edward W. Malley, Jr.
and his wife Barbara,
under whose merry roof
this story was written.

Lengthwise was a bookworm who made his home in a dictionary.

He began life among the A's and started nibbling right away.

A-words were very tasty. They were flavored with printer's ink, and the paper had a crispy, crunchy crackle like cornflakes.

As he swallowed each A-word, Lengthwise digested its meaning. It wasn't long before he had tunneled his way from "an" to "at," having grown smarter and stronger with every bite.

Then one day Lengthwise reached the end of the A's, and he decided that he was now strong enough and smart enough to leave his bookshelf and go out into the world. So he left his dictionary home and crawled along the bookshelf until he came to an open window. Then over the sill and down the outside wall he went.

It was a long and difficult trip, but he made it.
When he reached the outside, Lengthwise looked
around. The day was cold and drizzly, but since he
had never been outdoors before, he felt satisfied and
cheerful. He ambled along the damp green grass until
his path was blocked by a plant whose name he knew
at once, for it was a plant that began with the letter
"a," an amaryllis.

9

Lengthwise climbed the amaryllis and sat down in its topmost blossom, which swayed like a tiny rocking chair in the breeze. From this dizzy height, he looked down at the garden. His eyes, which were round and darkly rimmed as if he wore black spectacles, grew wider with all he saw. What did he see?

He saw a sparrow on a bough, a butterfly hovering over a tulip, and an ant who was bringing a crumb to her family.

He didn't know what a sparrow was, or a butterfly. But when he saw the ant, he recognized her, for he had come across her name among the A's.

The ant, who was a friendly little creature, put down her crumb and stared at Lengthwise.

"Hi!" she said. "You're new around here, aren't you?"

"An accurate assumption!" replied Lengthwise, using A-words, which were all he had so far digested.

"Horrible weather we're having!" the ant continued.

"Aye, aye," Lengthwise replied. "Absolutely awful!"

"How funny you talk!" the ant exclaimed.

12

Lengthwise gazed at her wistfully. He wanted very much to be her friend. In fact, he wanted to ask her to go walking with him and share the many marvels in the garden. But how could he do this when all he knew were A-words?

Once more Lengthwise did his little best.

"Advance, amiable ant!" he began. "Amazing adventures await!"

"Good gracious!" said the ant. "What a show-off!" And she picked up her crumb and scurried away.

"Adieu!" said Lengthwise sadly.

13

Feeling puzzled and hurt, Lengthwise crawled up the wall and over the sill. He returned to his dictionary thinking that perhaps A's were not quite enough to have under his belt and that he would most certainly have to have a few B's before he could visit the garden again.

Many weeks passed as he tunneled his way through the pages. B-words were delightful. Lengthwise enjoyed them so much that he nibbled steadily from "baa" to "buzz." By the time he had digested "Byzantium," he felt strong enough and smart enough to go again into the wide, wide world. So once more he sought the open window and crawled down the outside wall.

Back in the garden, the little bookworm found to his amazement that everything looked different. This was because the sun was shining. Grass and moss were astir with busy bugs, all talking excitedly together. How he wished he knew what they were saying! At last he spied a bug whom he recognized at once. It was a beetle. He had come across the word "beetle" not long ago.

"Beautiful big black beetle," he burst out in a
flurry of lately-digested B-words, "behold a backward
bookworm!"

"Huh?" gasped the beetle. "Why all the big words,
pal?"

Lengthwise took a deep breath and tried again.
"Beautiful big black beetle, befriend a befuddled bookworm baffled by bewildering bug-babble!"

Like the ant, the beetle thought Lengthwise was a show-off. Disgusted, he dove into a rose and pulled its petals over him.

Poor Lengthwise wondered what he should do now. He had just about decided to return to the dictionary when a boy entered the garden. Under his arm he carried a geography book. He opened the book and sat down under a tree to study his lesson. Lengthwise crawled close.

"Boy!" he said. "Brave bright boy bearing beautiful big book, befriend a bewildered bookworm."

The boy did not hear him; he continued reading.
Lengthwise noticed he did not swallow the words on
the page. He seemed to nibble them with his eyes.

"Bye-bye, boy," said Lengthwise.

Since neither beetle nor boy paid any attention to him, Lengthwise returned to his bookshelf and started chewing again. Many days passed as he went from the C-section to the M's. He liked M-words immensely.

"Mmmmm!" he murmured happily.

He nibbled M-words until he could hold no more. Then out he went again for another adventure in the garden.

But what was wrong? Where *was* the garden? He thought it had disappeared, but it was nighttime, and the garden was lost in shadows.

Suddenly something round and silvery peeped from behind a cloud.

"Moon!" Lengthwise whispered. "Marvelous mellow moon!"

Awed, he continued to stare up at the sky. He had never seen the stars before. He didn't even know they *were* stars, for he had not yet come to the S-section in the dictionary.

Then a tiny light twinkled in the bushes. Length-wise thought at first that one of the lights in the sky must have fallen to earth. But it was not a falling star. It was only a firefly.

"Miraculous midget meteor!" exclaimed Length-wise.

The firefly's light blinked nervously.

"Big words frighten me," he said.

"Mortification makes me miserable," apologized Lengthwise.

The light in the bushes went out. It was obvious that the firefly did not want to be his friend.

Poor Lengthwise didn't know how he had failed. He sat himself down on a stone and thought about it. It must be that he had not eaten *enough* words. Yes, that was it. He must go back to the dictionary and eat more. In fact, he would not stop eating words until he had eaten the very last one. And so he returned to his dictionary and ate his way right through to the Z's.

It was then that the trouble began. Z-words did not agree with Lengthwise. They had sharp corners which scratched as they went down. He turned white when he swallowed "zigzag"; it was almost more than he could bear. Hoping to take the taste from his mouth, he hastily gobbled "zucchini," and that was his final mistake.

His eyes grew cloudy, his skin became damp, and his body began to tremble. He lost his grip on the page and tumbled out of the dictionary and onto the shelf.

Now I will surely die, he thought. But he didn't die. He slowly regained his strength and crawled weakly to the garden to get some air, and there he lay, curled up in pain.

Not far off, an elf sat on a moss-covered stone doing a crossword puzzle. Hearing the bookworm's groans, he glanced up.

"What's the matter?" he asked. "Are you sick?"

"Zounds!" exclaimed Lengthwise. "I've lost my zest. My zip has come unzipped."

But even with unzipped zip, Lengthwise was now able to use all the words he had digested.

"How funny you talk," said the elf. "You sound as though you've swallowed a dictionary."

"I did," said Lengthwise. "That's the trouble with me."

"Hmmm!" said the elf. "If you've swallowed a dictionary, perhaps you can help me with my cross-word puzzle."

"I know lots of cross words," Lengthwise replied. " 'Don't' is a cross word and 'won't' is a cross word, too —especially if you say it in a cross tone of voice."

28

"That's not what I mean," said the elf. "I've been working on this puzzle all day, and I can't go any further. I can't find the word that fits into this space. See?"

Lengthwise studied the puzzle. "The word is 'knowledge,'" he said, and he spelled it out for the elf.

The elf was very grateful.

"You've helped me a lot," he said. "Now, how may I help *you*? You were unhappy being a bookworm. Would you like to be something else? How would you like to be a lion?"

"No, thanks," said Lengthwise. "I'd be afraid of myself."

"What about an elephant?" suggested the elf. "Or a zebra, maybe?"

"No." Lengthwise shook his head sadly.

"Wait a minute," said the elf. "I have an idea. You helped me with a word I needed; maybe you can do the same for someone else. We wouldn't have to change you into anything. Would you like that?"

"Oh, yes, more than anything," replied Lengthwise. "What is your idea?"

"I know a man who is an author. Sometimes when he is writing a story, he has a very hard time thinking of just the right word he needs in a certain place. You could live with him and help him."

Lengthwise was very happy. "Let's do it right away," he said.

31

And that is exactly what happened. Lengthwise, the bookworm, went to live with Mr. Wright, the author, who also loved words. He was a bespectacled man, the bookworm type.

They became friends immediately, and that very day they set to work on a story.

From that time on, Mr. Wright dedicated every book he wrote: "To my friend L." And nobody but Mr. Wright knew that the "L" was for Lengthwise.